The Garden

the GARDEN

a bouquet of stories & sonnets

Mackenzie Lynn

Foreword by Tess Cunningham

Illustrations & Design by Ashley VanArsdale Parmenter

Here's to the stubborn and hard-headed girls: may you flex until everyone knows that you are strong, scream until your voice is heard, and fight until your battle is won.

contents

*"She was not fragile like a flower,
she was fragile like a bomb."*

– Frida Kahlo

foreword

When two flowers are planted side by side in a garden, it is a given circumstance that they will remain there, rooted and together, for all their lives. Because flowers, of course, can grow—they bloom, and they must acknowledge the passage of time—but they cannot really change. They are embedded, dependent upon their beginnings, and so they cannot leave their gardens. Two people, of course, are not so simple. We can be planted together and grow together, but unlike flowers, we are granted the ability to grow on the inside, too. So people, over time, will change remarkably. And, people, over time, will start to leave their gardens. So, it's not every lifetime you get to grow with someone, together, for your entire life. But, every once in a while, two people will get very lucky, and even after they leave that garden they shared as children, they will continue growing towards the same sun, so that they may always share each other's company.

I count myself so lucky. A lifelong friend is something remarkably sacred. Can you really tackle life's greatest mysteries—heartbreaks, tragedies, and beautiful wonders alike—with the same person you tackled primary colors with? Sometimes. Often life starts to get tangled up in itself, and you have to tie off pieces of the past into neat little ribbons in order to keep moving forward. Sometimes, though, it works out that you just need your person—the one who's seen it all, who needs no crash courses or backstories, and who can handle any curve ball you might throw at them. And goodness knows Mackenzie has seen all my tricks: we graduated kindergarten, high school, and college together. I call her mom "Mom," and I'm pretty sure I've gross-cried on both of them. I'd let her read my diary, if I had one, but she wouldn't need to; she was there. We have seen each other at our worst—and our best—and so I feel incredibly privileged to watch her continually growing ever closer to her sun.

Here, I will risk being too on-the-nose, but I put too much subconscious thought into this not to share it: If I had to compare my friend to one flower, it would be the French Hydrangea. First, because they are beautiful and widely beloved; second, because they are perennials, always finding a way; and third, because they possess a unique ability to bloom in different colors based on the acidity of their soil. This last point may seem overly metaphorical, but bear with me: there are many plants that wouldn't be able to grow at all in such varied conditions, and others still that would pull through, but with a degree of uncertainty. And then there's the hydrangea, who says, "Yes, I'm different in this garden than I was in that one. It suits me now, don't you think? And just wait until you see me next year." See, my friend adapts to her surroundings, but she also makes her surroundings adapt back. I've always been inspired by her ability to hit the ground running, and I don't think I've ever seen a hurdle stop her more than temporarily. If anything, setbacks seem to spur her momentum (and Mackenzie, if that's not the case, you are the literal queen of fake-it-til-you-make-it, which is still a hell of an accomplishment). I like to think that, over the years, I've picked up some of her fire. I definitely find myself using it as a pilot light, at the very least.

It must be said, then, that I am so proud of this book's author; I am proud of the person she is, I am proud of the person she has been, and I already know that I will be proud of the many versions of herself she is yet to become. When she first told me about her idea for The Garden, I knew right away it would be a turning point for her. This is the kind of project that builds in you day by day until it finally becomes too grand to contain, and even then it takes a steady hand to actually sculpt art from our emotions as they burst out of us. I was eager, but I didn't know what to expect. Then, when she sent me an early draft to read, I wanted to call just about every woman I'd ever known. Look at this, I wanted to say, and tell me which page feels most like a mirror. That's how it felt for me, anyway: like I was looking into the warped glass of a fun house maze, seeing dozens of versions of a story I had lived. The faces were blurred, and the details were fuzzy, but the concepts remained clear.

I then felt a mix of liberation and pain, relief and rage, as I realized that I was not alone in the maze. I wished the fun house were empty—that our art needn't drip with the venom we were only trying to return. I wished that my friend didn't know these stories, but she did. She knew them, and she knew how to make them her own again.

I hope that every reader finds within this book the combination of peace and power they need to keep growing. I hope, too, that every living being on this garden we call Earth finds the peace and power within ourselves to make our world a more loving place; there are all kinds of mirror mazes out there, filled with all kinds of stories, and we are all responsible for helping each other out.

Mackenzie, it is no surprise that you have created something wonderful. I cannot wait to keep growing with you.

Tess Cunningham,
Artist, Friend, and Probable Dandelion

the garden

What causes us flowers to grow?
Is it the seeds or the soil or the sun in the sky?
What causes us to look so dreary?
What causes us to die?

Do you know what we do?
We provide homes to the bees and the butterflies.
We clean the air around you,
And yet some people are not so kind.

Some just don't notice,
Little boys pick us and break off the roots,
Some people don't appreciate us,
Some walk on us in their boots.

But that is not the worst part,
The people who hurt us until we shatter,
It is the ones who only see our beauty,
Those that treat us like that is all that matters.

Oh, yes, we are pretty,
But there is so much else that we provide,
Here in The Garden,
We work with pride.

Each of us is different,
But please don't compare,
We work together,
Don't pick a favorite, oh don't you dare.

Without all of us,
The Garden would not grow,
And sure, your eyes would not notice,
But the earth would definitely know.

So, you can bend us,
Tear us, yes, break us apart,
But just because you're angry,
You cannot fix your broken heart.

For the people who only love what they see,
Do not understand that there is more than meets the eye.
Without these pretty flowers,
There would not be birds in the sky.

If you stomp on us and crush us,
Sure, we won't be so appealing,
But we are not just a sight,
We are more than just a feeling.

You use us and cut us off,
To put in a vase for your wives,
You look at us until we wither,
And you eventually end our lives.

Oh, please rest assured,
That is not the end of the road,
Our seeds will fall,
And a new flower grows.

You don't have to plant the seed,
For our population to prosper,
For these so-called delicate flowers,
Oh, we have so much more to offer.

While our scent is sweet,
Our revenge is not sour,
We will continue to flourish,
We will gain power.

Daisy

Straight A's. Class President. Boss babe.

Tell me, how does one separate her boobs from her brain?

The fall of my junior year of college was one of the most exciting periods of my entire life. Opportunities were coming at me from all angles. Interviews and phone calls and office visits seemed to be a weekly occurrence as I was looking for a summer internship. I had options. I had the opportunity to say no.

So why did I say "yes" to this?

An interview with a large financial planning company came my way and I felt honored. This internship was well-respected. It was named a Top Ten internship in the country for finance, and the selection process for interns, I was told, was grueling and as competitive as possible.

When I walked into the doors, Fox News was playing in the lobby. One woman was in the office. She was the receptionist. A man came up to me who reminded me of a football coach. He shook my hand and led me to the conference room, where our hour-long interview would take place.

My research told me that this would be the first interview of several. I sat down and the interview began.

"Did you play sports in high school? You look like an athlete."

"Yes, I was a swimmer, and I played volleyball."

"Oh, thank God. I was worried that you were a cheerleader."

"No, I played volleyball and swam."

"Great, you do not seem like most millennials. Do you like to talk on the phone?"

"Yes, I pride myself in my ability to converse in-person and on the phone without relying much on text messaging."

"Great. Well, I feel confident enough right now, and believe me we *never* do this, but I want you to intern with us. Do you accept?"

Without hesitation, I agreed. I thought about how proud my family would be of me. I thought about how my resume would shine in comparison to those of my peers.

He walked me through the cubicles of the office and introduced me to his colleagues. Prior to meeting the branch manager, he looked at me with urgency.

"Now, if you tell *anyone* that I hired you without all of the formalities of making you do a sales pitch and doing six more interviews, my boss will have my hide. Don't say anything, okay?"

Still feeling honored, I kept his promise and acted like I was held to the standards this company was known for enforcing.

As the spring semester went by, I became licensed for life and health insurance brokerage, and started attending classes and seminars that would prepare me for my prestigious internship. When I talked to some of my peers and mentors about the internship, they warned me about the things that they had heard.

"You will not make much money."

"It is a scam."

"That internship has a dirty little secret."

I brushed off the advice and eagerly approached the office the May of my internship.

I lived in a townhouse with four strangers in order to save money. My rent plus utilities was $350 a month and I was guaranteed $400 a month from my internship. This did not concern me, because I knew in no time that I would have hundreds if not thousands of dollars in commissions. But I started moonlighting as a hostess at a local seafood restaurant just in case.

When I met the other members of the internship class, I was excited. In my office, there were nine interns total and two of us were women. I could tell that we all would get along just fine.

Things began to take a turn when I realized the environment in the office was more of a boy's club than I had anticipated. Men in the office would joke that they "majored in football" and really only made the grades they needed in order to play in that week's game.

I turned 21 during my internship, and when I showed up to work, many were surprised.

"Why are you even here? You realize it is your 21st birthday? You should be puking your guts out in an alley somewhere."

"Well, it is a Thursday, so I am celebrating this weekend."

The agent who interviewed me came up to me with a wine cooler.

"You just got iced. I got you something fruity, since I figured you were a girl and didn't like beer."

I was expected to drink the bottle while taking a knee in the middle of the office. I mean, of course I was since there was a fridge full of beer in the office anyway. Instead, I took it home and drank the watermelon concoction before bed.

As the internship went by, I realized that the other interns were talking about their interview processes. I laughed to myself when I would hear that they were forced to do more interviews than I was. I assumed it was because they saw potential in me that the others did not possess.

It wasn't until the other female intern came up to me that I had even thought about questioning the process.

"I only had one interview. How about you?"

"Umm yeah, me too."

Could it be that we were hired because we were women? In the state, there were over 100 interns with only nine females. Each of us only had one interview.

Annual conference was an incentive for those of us interns
who met our sales goals. The four of us who made the cut
drove in a minivan down to Alabama excited to see what this
meeting had in store. Little did we know, it was a weekend of
drinking, sharing beds and watching our agents have affairs
with the human resources female staff members.

The "incentive" that meant to be an opportunity for us,
meant other things for the salesmen.

"We HATE bringing our wives here. It is not even a vacation
when they are here."

"I booked hotel rooms for all of you, but you will have to
share beds. Girls do not mind that right? I got extra cots
for the men."

My concerns were pushed aside throughout the entire
internship. I liked the freedom I had. I went to the office
when I wanted. I was never required to do anything.
My weekly stipend was $100 that would later be
taxed heavily.

I was honored, but in hindsight, I see why people warned me.

The soundtrack of the office filled with sexist comments was enough for me.

"You are doing really well in this internship. It is probably because of how cute you are."

"His wife is a professional cheerleader. She is a total bimbo, but who cares since she is so hot."

"You are all very lucky to be here. Many people went through interview after interview to have a spot in your shoes and they did not get an offer."

Poppy

I am easy.
Easy to love
But easy to leave.

He is a chase.
Someone you earn
And yearn for.

I am loyal.
Going nowhere,
Unconditional.

He is a prize.
Go away with him,
And leave everyone else behind.

Why do men do that?

Seriously, why does it always feel this way?

My friends get in a relationship with someone who demands all of them. Their time. Their effort. Their patience.

And I get tossed to the wayside.

Given that I am not paying for all their dates or sleeping with them, I kind of get it. But I am fun. I am loyal. I am fairly low maintenance. You won't have to choose between me and another friend. We could go months without talking, and I still would pick up the phone the moment you and that loser broke up.

I just don't get it.

My friends pick true winners. I mean *real winners*.

For example, one of my friends dated this guy who literally made fun of her. Told her that she was not that attractive. Not like a teasing way. Like a true "you're ugly" way. But because he was laughing and she loved him, she let it slide.

Meanwhile, if I do not tell her "Happy Birthday" right at midnight, something is wrong. Because I am the friend who has every detail of your special day lined up. I will take you axe throwing. I will drive into the night just so you can see the Grand Canyon for the first time if that is what you asked. I would do anything to see you smile.

But somehow, that doesn't work. Because you do not have to work for me. I cannot make you smile the way that you do when the man who never woos you one day tells you that you are pretty. The way you grin when he finally pops the question after you got your hopes up date after date that it would happen.

I truly bend over backwards for someone who bends over backwards for someone else.

I get it. I am easy.

But how is it that someone who accepts nothing but the best in her life in every other facet chooses to be with someone who is not even half the man that she deserves?

Somedays, I wish I was a boy. That way, I could take her on a date. I could be some random blind date that she was set up with. I would open every door. I would pull her chair out for her. I would tell her how amazing she is, and how everything she does is pure magic. How she deserves nothing but the absolute best.

Truthfully, my friend is competitive.

She sees a man who, on the surface, is a bit repulsive. He is not the kind of guy that you bring home to your parents. He isn't particularly nice, and your dad will most definitely not approve. He will tell you to jump and you will, for whatever reason ask, "how high?" He could ask you to run away with him—abandon this current life in pursuit of his dreams—and you will go looking for your suitcase.

But she sees a dusty and corroded rock; one that she believes she can turn into something resembling a diamond. With enough pressure and maybe the right environment, the rock becomes shiny. It will cut her with every attempt to polish, and it will make her life a mess. She will focus her energy on making that rock shine. She no longer thinks about her hobbies. She doesn't do what she wants. Her friends will be there if he isn't, but that doesn't matter right now.

All that matters is she wins.

She proves all of the naysayers wrong.

Her rock gives her a diamond and the effort and scars will be, in her eyes, worth it.

And yet, why?

Why do we as women toss everyone else aside but these turds of human beings? Like there is some award at the pearly gates for "woman who threw away all of her hopes and dreams to win over a man who really doesn't care" and God says "good job, way to deal with my greatest test." And all of the other exhausted women put her on their shoulders as they compare how little their boyfriends cleaned, how often their husbands complained, or how long they waited for their partner to commit.

I won't do that; I would rather wait than settle.

Someday, I hope that my person comes to me. I hope that he is currently living his best life and that he is working hard to make his hopes and dreams come true. I hope he isn't lost looking for me, but that we stumble upon each other by accident, or maybe just when we are ready.

And I pray that he treats me the way I believe my friend deserves to be treated. Because God knows that women don't look out for themselves like we do our best friends.

How we watch our friends in horrible relationships and ask why they stay, and yet we go home to the same passionless and indifferent marriages. How we would find the best man that we could find to set them up with our sisters, but we wouldn't take that man for ourselves.

I pray that I love myself long enough to no longer believe that I am worthy of anything less than a man with the charm that will make my mom happy, the respect that will shake my dad's hand, and the heart that will make mine skip a beat.

And I pray that you will, too.

weeds

Flowers. Flawless flowers
Filling gardens full of fuchsia
Flooding rooms with fun

Flowers. Powerless flowers
Left rooted to the floor
Stuck standing on the soil to be stomped

Flowers. Growing flowers
Seeds sprouting into blooms
Stems shooting into sky

Flowers. Sad flowers
Annuals attempting to shine to expiration
Perennials looking down upon them

Flowers. Delicate flowers
Taught to choose us because we smell nice
Picking us but at what price

Flowers. Voiceless flowers
Rose and Daisy do their best
Mike and Tom still rise above the rest

Flowers. Trampled flowers
Rose and Daisy reach for sun
Mike and Tom have already won

Iris

Nice guy, "I am a nice guy," he sings,
Constant smiles and laughs ring,
Nice guy, "I am a nice guy," he shouts,
When anyone shows a sign of doubt.

"What do you mean? I don't understand?" he's perplexed.
A man's privilege is suddenly so complex.
"I don't see sex, I don't see race, I don't see color."
Oh, I get it, you truly do not even bother.

Being blind means that you cannot see,
All that I am, all that I can, all that I bring,
Being blind means you turn your head,
To all that I suffer, all that I endure, all that I dread.

Walk a mile in my shoes,
Try even around the block,
Instead, reduce me to nothing,
My troubles you mock.

"But I am a good guy!
Why do you accuse?"
You are not a bad person,
Just try on my shoes.

I worked hard. No, I worked my butt off. Long days turned into long nights for weeks on end preparing for this presentation. All for my efforts to be overshadowed by the control hungry attitude of my boss.

As a new-ish employee in a renowned consulting company, I no doubt had to pay my dues to prove my worth. And I was prepared to do that.

A new client with a lot of potential and opportunity came across my screen. I made my introductions and ended up being their primary provider for marketing and sales resources. I was ecstatic. Without even stepping foot in their office, I was able to make them trust me.

Don't get me wrong, I knew that I would get it. I studied and researched and planned every step of the way to get there. Before I even picked up the phone, I knew that I would have a fully committed client by the time I hung up.

I crushed it.

The only box left to check off was to do a field visit. I needed to simply show up, shake some hands, and solidify the partnership.

If I wasn't confident before, I was even more so now.

Ronda Rousey once said that she would beat any other fighter because she was more prepared than any other competitor. She spent more time training than her opponent, so she knew that she was more ready. I did the same thing.

What Rousey did not mention was that it was possible for someone to come up from behind her, break her leg, and take away her chance to fight. Like Nancy Kerrigan, someone could steal every hour that was spent preparing from her—leaving both her leg and her heart shattered as she looks up at the traitor on the podium.

If only someone told me.

For this field visit, my manager thought it would be a great opportunity to complete an evaluation of my abilities.

Perfect.

I thought about how this would be a great way for me to prove myself. I wanted him to see how hard I worked. I wanted him to know that I was ready to kill it.

If only someone told me.

The morning of the visit, my boss met me at the office to make the short drive over to the client.

"You excited?" He asked me as I went through my presentation notes.

"Yeah! Let's go!" I replied.

I knew that this would be an awesome meeting.

We get out of the car and walk into the building. My boss walks directly in front of me to introduce himself to every person in the room.

First red flag.

I shake the hands of the men that I had been working with for weeks.

"Hey, it's nice to put a face to a name," I keep things light. Smiles on all the faces around as we walk into the warehouse. I began to see all the product that I was promoting. It was all coming together.

We walk into the back office of the building and meet the

leadership team. Before I can even say my name, my manager cuts me off and introduces himself.

Second red flag.

He has always been a bit of a social butterfly, but come on? This is my thing. Just sit down and watch.

If only someone told me.

I began my presentation by offering the executives an opportunity to ask questions. This group of men in their fifties and sixties were full of questions regarding social media and search engine optimization. I was ready to show them how educated and capable I was to continue to promote their business.

Their questions begin.

"So how is the market looking for ad sales right now? Will we have to expand our methods?"

Easy answer.

"So glad you asked that. I—."

"Well you know," He cut me off. My manager stole my first question. He answers with years more experience and technical jargon that makes even the SAT vocabulary look elementary.

Second question arrives.

"Awesome! How is our awareness? Are we fairly visible on Facebook right now?"

Again, another easy answer. A response I had prepared for nights.

"We are doing—."

"I know that this business…" HE DID IT AGAIN. Steals my thunder.

And then, the biggest, boldest, and reddest flag. A flag that the most successful matador would wave to entice their bull.

"Hey, write that down. You need to take notes." My manager looks at me and tells me to assume the role of secretary at a meeting THAT I PLANNED.

Memories of business school flashed through my head. Female professors telling me to never take notes for a room full of men. Strong women that told me to be assertive.

And there I was, the only one prepared to take notes. In a room full of all men, I am the only one who thought that bringing a pen and paper would be useful. And I am punished for it.

Sorry Ronda, being prepared shot me in the foot.

The rest of the visit was pretty much me following my boss and the executive team throughout the warehouse as they had conversations about how our company could further capitalize on marketing. How we would make their business even more successful. I did not get to open my mouth but was instead told to take notes. All of my time spent preparing was wasted. A man with more experience in the industry took my spotlight. He didn't even know what that company did until I told him on the drive to the meeting.

It didn't matter.

The visit ended, and we walked to the company car.

"That went super well. Great job." My manager gives me a pat on the back.

Cool. A kudos.

A week went by and my boss gets an email from my client asking a question. Going over my head, they email my manager. I was not even CC'd.

I go home that night furious.

He stole my thunder.

He robbed me of my credibility.

He ruined my relationship with a client that I knew so well. A partnership that I worked so hard to foster.

I walk into the office the next day and decided to talk to my boss about the situation.

"Look, I know that this was not the intention, but because you told me to take notes, I have lost credibility with my client."

"Yeah, I know, I am sorry. But they seem to like us! Lots of potential!"

I continue.

"I know that you did not realize this, but I was the only woman in the room. And you asked me to take notes. That is not cool."

"Why? Why bring that up?" He seemed defensive.

"Well, it is an example of benevolent sexism. If you needed to borrow a pen, you could have just asked instead of assuming that I would take notes."

"I don't understand. Do you think I am sexist? I don't see race. I don't see sex. I don't see gender. Seriously??!"

This was a lost cause to say the least.

Weeks continued and I was suddenly taking notice of his lack of awareness.

Concerns from female coworkers about the business were met with "Wow, you nag like my wife."

Luncheons with directors from other offices just so happened to only include the salesmen and not the saleswomen.

Conversations constantly revolved around fraternity parties in college, and how his wife was so upset when he showed up to their wedding hungover.

Class act.

Needless to say, I know better now.

I still prepare like crazy.

I work hard.

But I always hide my pen and paper.

Jasmine

Growing up, all I wanted was a husband.

And now I have one.

So, tell me,

If all my dreams have come true,

Why am I not happy?

It was the first day of my sophomore year in high school. I walked into the gym teacher's office to discuss ultimate frisbee club, and he walked in behind me. Not just anyone, but the man that I knew I would one day call my husband.

He was tall and handsome. His goofy laugh paired with his contagious grin left me wondering if there was any way that he could possibly break my heart.

We never officially dated in high school. We did go to prom together as friends and became frequent teammates on our coed frisbee team.

We hung out in our tight clique of choir kids and band freaks. The people who wanted to be active, but really didn't want to try out for basketball or swim. I felt like the tension could be cut with a knife. I wanted him badly. But somehow, I was always too scared to tell him how I felt.

I would like to say things have changed.

It is crazy to think that I am truly afraid of anything. I have rappelled off the side of cliffs in the Rockies. I have jumped from the high dive at the local university pool. I have ridden the tallest and fastest of roller coasters. I even drove cross-country on Friday the 13th in the middle of a hailstorm. I fear nothing.

And yet, my husband has all the power over me.

When I ask myself what I'm afraid of, I begin to laugh. Looking at him, no one could possibly be scared. His Birkenstocks and jean shorts with a Grateful Dead t-shirt coming at you in an alley would not leave you feeling like you would be held at gunpoint. You might think he would offer you a piece of gum or ask if you needed anything.

And yet, my husband has all the power over me.

Truly, there are many different reasons I am afraid.

Is it because I am not happy?

I know that he doesn't mean to be a bad partner in my life, but he is constantly telling me what he likes about me in ways that make it seem as though the alternative is heinous. Like "I like your hair curled a lot" when he sees me with my hair thrown in its typical messy bun. Or when he says that my favorite artist is not that great. Or when he tells me that my friends are not that great, even though they have been there for me in times when he has been miles away.

Is it because the idea of being married to him was more exciting than actually being married to him?

I feel like there is usually a period after the wedding when the honeymoon phase is over, and you just wonder if this is it. Is this the rest of our lives? Like how long until we have kids, raise them, retire, move to Florida, and just die already? Was I just excited about the glam of the wedding? The ball gowns and up-do's and catering and photos, and all the people there telling me that I look so beautiful. Honestly, it was not that big of a deal. I had more people passively congratulating me on Facebook than I did in the church on the day I said, "I do".

Is it because all I ever wanted was to be wanted and now, I do not feel that way at all?

Like now that I have your last name, is the chase over? Do we just sit? No more games of tag on cell phones from states away when you were just out of reach. Now that you have me, do you even want me? Like, if I walked out the door tomorrow, would you even try to stop me?

Is it because I had every opportunity to give someone else a chance?

Jesse in accounting. Matt from church. Isaiah in my management class. All of them. Rejected. And now, I am with someone who I had to wear down.

Or is it because I would have to go back to each of my friends, the ones I pushed out of my life along this broken road to wifedom, only to tell them that I was wrong?

I felt like all my closest friends were walking on eggshells around me about my relationship. Like, they all thought I was waiting around for something that was not going to happen. Or, that I was missing out on life in front of me simply because I wanted to be a wife so badly. Most of them I do not even recognize anymore. Our lives have all changed so drastically, and we feel the need to talk about the weather when all we did before was discuss our rawest moments. How could I tell them that I am sorry? How could I say, "you're right" and that I have changed?

So here I am, lips zipped, waiting for the day we pack our bags and begrudgingly move to Florida.

briars

That is not a compliment.

Referring to me as the "best looking salesperson" in the office.

That is not a compliment.

Telling me that even though I did not get the job, I would likely make a good mother someday.

That is not a compliment.

Drawing your eyes down my body as you tell me that I did a good job on that presentation.

That is not a compliment.

Saying that "despite being a woman" I can be assertive.

That is not a compliment.

Mouthing to me that my legs look great in my skirt as I walk up on the stage for a speaking engagement.

That is not a compliment.

Putting your arm around me as you come to my desk to tell me how glad you are that we are working together.

That is not a compliment.

If you would not say it to your brother,
do not say it to me.

Ivy

What a waste, what a loss,
To see a woman sleep with her boss
Her intention was for love and passion,
His was to hold her accountable for her actions

What a shame, oh how sad,
When the woman seems so glad,
A new promotion, an office with a view,
For a favor to her boss was due

What is so obvious? Was the door shut?
When whispered water cooler words shout "slut"
He keeps his reputation though,
And she's the victim of quid pro quo

What should she do? What can be done?
When a woman is only seen as "fun"
What about her hustle? What about her brain?
You've never seen a pay raise cause so much pain

Oh, what a pity? Oh, this is bad,
Divorces end dreams they never had,
True colors are shown, and "favors" never end,
This initial affair becomes a tragic trend

What a mistake, what a regret,
The heat of the moment she'll never forget,
For her career is on hold, a dreadful pause,
All because she slept with her boss

After one year at my company, I went from the lowest position in the department to training marketing executives. I was not smarter. I was not more qualified. In fact, some people that I was technically training had years more experience, a better way with clients, and some had professional degrees from the best business schools in the country.

And yet, I was technically in charge of them.

My name is Ivy, and this is my story.

As a college senior, I was bright-eyed and ready for the future. I practically had "boss" tattooed on my forehead as I breezed through each and every interview. No one could say no to me.

A company that is well respected in my industry called me for an interview in their downtown office. I show up with my best blazer, the one that Elle Woods would have worn her first time in the courtroom. I walked into the office, shook hands, aced their questions, and unsurprisingly, I received a phone call with an offer the next morning. I was ecstatic. Many of my friends did not even hear back, let alone get an offer.

Three weeks after graduation, I started my job in the office. I worked hard, learned as much as I possibly could, and put my best foot forward each and every day. The people I worked with enjoyed my company, and I quickly made friends. This wasn't particularly shocking, since I was a Rho Gam in college. I was practically made to make friends.

The people that I supported oversaw the largest accounts in my office. I mostly did data entry for them and made many phone calls to ensure that their operations were working smoothly.

My manager was honestly the nicest and funniest person in the office. He seemed a bit shy, and as a social butterfly, I saw it as a challenge to make sure that he came out of his shell. Many days, I made him laugh and would poke fun at him. Eventually, he would fire back at me with some sarcastically goofy reply. Mission accomplished.

The parking garage for the office was located three blocks down the street. Before and after work, many of us would walk together to our cars through the alley.

One day, my manager stopped me as I was walking out the door.

"Hey Ivy, wait for me."

I stood in the entryway, as he put his coat on, and we made our way out of the building.

"Did you have a good day?"

"Sure, I had a great day. Did you?" I replied.

"Yeah I did."

We continued walking down the alley.

"Ugh, my wife is a hag." He was looking at his phone that showed three missed calls, followed by a text from his wife telling him to call her on his way home.

He continued. "I bet you are really good to your husband."

"Umm, yeah I am!"

We reached the garage. As I began to walk away, he said that he would like to walk together again.

The next day after work, he continued confiding in me about troubles with his wife. She apparently was a nurse and worked many shifts that offset with his own schedule, which left him to watch their kids.

"I shouldn't have to babysit all of the time, you know?"

Honestly, I could somewhat understand. My husband traveled monthly out of state for work, and I felt alone and tired many days. I told him that, though I did not have kids, I did have to do a lot of the work at home since my husband was away often.

We walked up the stairs in the parking garage, and he thanked me for letting him vent.

"We should do this at lunch, too. I'll buy!" He offered.

"Sounds great. See you tomorrow."

Weeks went by, and we created quite a friendship. We felt very comfortable with one another, and I honestly felt a connection with him. With my husband being gone, and his wife working nights, we needed each other. When I would cry anytime my husband left, my manager would give me a tight hug and grab my hand.

Then it happened.

One day at lunch, he asked if I would walk to his car with him since he forgot his wallet. We got to his car, and he said that he would actually drive to lunch since it was cold out.

I sat in the passenger side, and before I could even open my mouth, he kissed me.

And I liked it. I liked it a lot.

Our hands moved quickly, and my heart pounded fast. When something was so wrong, why did it just get hotter?

By the end of lunch hour, the car had not moved an inch. Neither of us bought food, and it was time to head back to the office.

From that point on, our conversations were very different. He talked to me like my manager until we were making out.

One week later, he called me into his office.

"Do you have any interest in a promotion?" he asked.

I could not have been happier. I was working two jobs and was waiting for this. I did not expect it to happen until I brought it up, but I was excited.

The next day, I began working as a Marketing Executive. I had my own accounts and was grinding harder than ever.

Life was so good.

Until a few months later when my husband came home and said he wanted to see me more. He was potentially getting a promotion and would have to work in another state.

Luckily, my company had offices in other cities, so the ability to transfer was an option.

I talked to my manager the next day. We sat in his office, and I knew that I had to end things.

"You are going to leave me? How are you going to get a job out there?" he asked.

"Well, I was planning to have my job in another office if possible." I was sure that he would vouch for me, since he was the one who promoted me in the first place.

"Oh honey, you really think that will happen? Will your husband want you there when he finds out that you are sleeping with me?" His voice seemed like he pitied me with its condescending tone.

I was stunned. Was I being blackmailed? He leaned forward

and shook me to my core.

"You really think that you can flirt your way to the top again? You cannot make moves on every manager you have."

He looked at me as though my intentions were to sleep my way to the top. Who was he kidding? Did he suddenly forget my perky, go-get-'em demeanor that walked in the first day of work? The way that I included him in every office conversation just to bring him out of his shell?

Don't flatter yourself, dude. I am friendly to everyone. My resting nice face paired with my impulse to compliment people tends to give off an unintentional flirty vibe.

I was simply trying to be nice.

Besides. If he hadn't escorted me to his car, drove me to lunch, and reclined his passenger seat, we wouldn't be having this conversation.

By the end of it, my husband and I got divorced. I told him that I could not move offices, and I wanted him to be happy. Plus, I could not live in fear of my manager potentially blackmailing me.

Which is quite hysterical if you think about it. Like, how can someone who is doing the same thing as me use this situation as leverage while I am suddenly losing everything?

So yeah, I now have the corner office. But it is not because I earned it. At least not the way that I wanted to earn it. Each and every compliment I receive is tarnished by the feeling that it is a shot to hit on me versus actually considering my intellect.

If I could give advice to any woman in business, it would be to be cold. Be cold as ice. Give stony stares, and do not make any effort to be the bubbly girl in the office. If you do, every other person you work with will hate you, and you will constantly question whether or not you have earned any professional accolade that comes your way.

Rose

I thought you liked me,

Your x-ray eyes scanned me up and down,

I saw your heart,

You looked through my clothes and tore me apart.

Work was different that night. He was my supervisor. And he was *cute*. I knew that he was nearly twice my age. But I also knew that he made me laugh. Flirting was through the roof.

Ten minutes before the end of shift, he passed me a note. My heart skipped a beat.

"I need to ask you a question after work."

"Why can't you ask me now?"

"It has to be when everyone is gone, and you have clocked out."

"Okay."

He kept the paper, and we all got in line to clock out. My pulse heightened. My ears rang.

Everyone left as I waited in the vending-machine lit lobby. He came up to me and handed me the piece of paper.

"Send me a naked picture."

I looked up at him and laughed.

"You should probably buy me dinner first."

"Rip up the piece of paper and throw it away."

He left in a quiet rage, slightly embarrassed but mainly angry.

As I drove home, millions of feelings went through my mind.

Does he think I am cute? He is seriously 14 years older than me.

What will happen when I see him again? Will he ask me out? Will he apologize?

I told the manager what had happened. I couldn't get paid for the hours I could not work, but I was told to go to HR to talk to them.

HR called me in.

"What do you want to happen as a result of this meeting?"

What did I want to happen? I *wanted* to not believe that he was going to retaliate. I *wanted* to think that this did not happen. I *wanted* to not ever see him again.

"Well, I do not want him to lose his job."

I later quit my job, and he is still a supervisor.

thorns

Today, I dressed up nice
I never saw so many heads turn

Why did I feel good?
Why did I like the attention?

Imagine,
Life could be sweet if people turned heads
for my brain instead of my butt

Imagine,
The world would be more collaborative if
we could always be seen like this

Why did I feel uncomfortable?
Undressing me with your eyes from my
neck to my thighs

Imagine,
Being taken seriously at my job

Imagine,
Not feeling afraid of looking my best

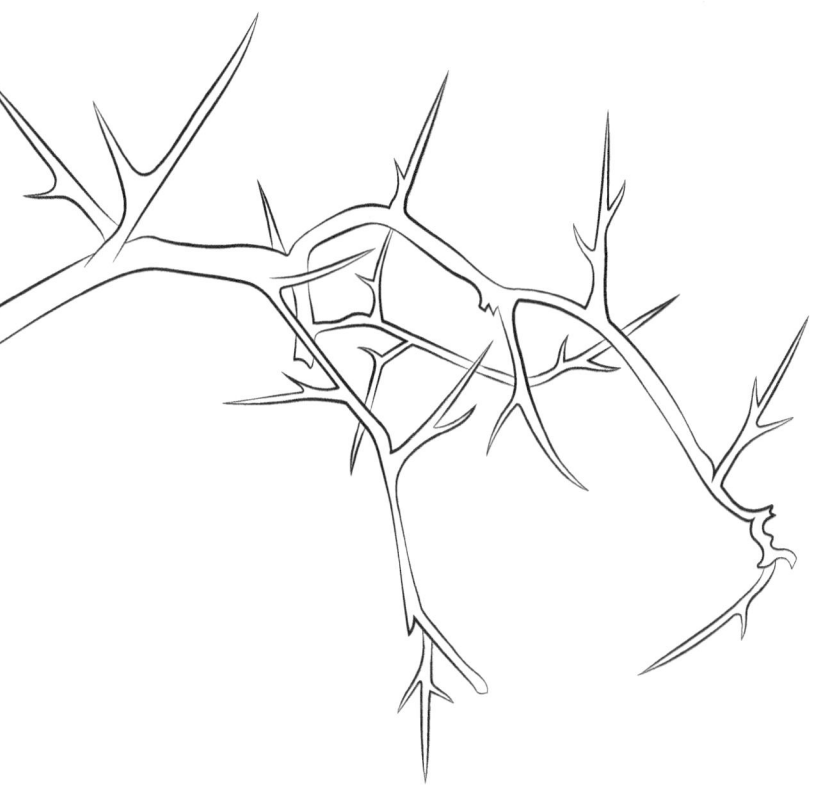

Am I more than my figure?
Am I more than my looks?
Did you even notice in my arms I was
carrying books?

Am I more than my body?
And am I more than my physique?
The things that caught your attention
aren't what make me unique

Imagine,
Waking up in the morning not wanting to
look your best

Imagine,
Afraid of putting on makeup because you
want to be heard not just seen

Am I more than my skin?
Am I more than my hair?
If you could only hear me, would you
know I was there?

Am I more than my thickness?
Am I more than my skirt?
Listen to a woman and get to know
her worth

Tomorrow,
I want to wear sweats and a ponytail
If Drake can see my worth, then why
won't Todd in accounting hear what
I have to say?

Violet

Seemingly perfect on paper

A real gentleman

4.0 GPA, athlete, crystal blue eyes

Your typical "good guy"

The type you bring home to the family

He is the best date in town

But from his perfect lips he's lying

And always bringing me down

What a total jerk. An utter piece of crap.

My name is Violet, and do I have a story for you.

It was a Tinder date with someone from my hometown that started this never-ending saga. We went to elementary school together as kids, but there was no way he remembered me.

But my gosh do I remember him. The nerdy athlete with the social awkwardness of the nearest 7th grader about to ask a girl to the dance.

I swiped right immediately.

A day later, he sends me a message asking to go on a date. I accept, trying to play it cool but really bursting at the seams.

Our date was perfect. Drinks and a walk around downtown. The night seemed to end with a kiss, until he asked me if I wanted to go to his apartment to see his photography from college. I was so excited to see his work and drove a half hour to his place at about 1am.

He immediately tries to get me in his bed.

"What are you doing?" I am shocked.

Turns out, he thought I would just hook up with him.

"I am not that easy," I tell him.

"Oh, I am sorry," he replies.

We talk that night and I go home. He asks me on another date, and I agree.

Dinner at a fancy restaurant with what appears to be a perfect guy.

This continues for weeks. Seeing each other a few days a week, but rarely answering texts. I usually had to have an excuse to see him.

I need a place to stay, my air conditioning is out.

My roommate brought her baby and she is crying. Can I stay with you?

Once he found out I was a virgin, things got even weirder.

You can stay but sleep on my couch.

I am going out of town the next few weekends.

The summer fling ended with a phone call.

I need to talk. You like me more than I like you. Sorry.

This "nice guy" really just led me on for three months. Never defined the relationship but met my family and went to a wedding with me.

Little did I know, he was seeing other people the entire time.

Fun fact: he isn't really a nice guy.

I like to call him a baker. Someone who has his cake and eats it too. Someone who is afraid to be honest, but not enough to respect you.

Dahlia

Is this love? Is this attention?

You're just one of the bad boys I hate to mention.

You hurt me and changed my mind.

You have made true love nearly impossible to find.

Once love is true, it's hard to say,

But I will likely push it all away.

He holds me tight and eases my pain.

"You will never be treated that way again."

I am the biggest fool on planet Earth.

Why? What happened to the girl with the highest standards? The one who broke up with boys who tried to pressure her? The one who checked her potential suitor's report card and resume before even seeing his face?

Everything changed. And all because of one man who gave her the attention that she once longed for.

My senior year of college was hectic. 23 credit hours per semester, working two jobs, and as I have jokingly referred to it, "raising a toddler."

This is not a stab at mothers in college, or even to say that my work was anywhere near that of a person who takes care of a child while chasing their dreams. Keep it up. You are crushing it.

This is a metaphor for the constant caring and keeping of a 27-year-old manchild. A person who would call in the middle of the night saying that he needed me. A person who told me that his life would not be worth living if I was not a part of it. A person who threatened to kill himself if I did not drop everything that I was doing in order to be in his arms.

People, this is not love. This is abuse. If you deal with this, *run for the hills*. Run far, far away until you forget why you ran. Live your life. Get out. Do not sacrifice even an ounce of who you are to be someone's better half.

This was not all. The abuse goes so much further. The sabotage came in all forms. Exposing himself to me behind the screen of my laptop while I was in a conference call with my boss and 30 colleagues, delivering a presentation that I spent hours preparing for. The use of a chainsaw in the apartment that I slept in. The passing out at dinner with family. The showing up to my college graduation party two hours late with a bottle of tequila and bar t-shirt in hand. You know, since those are the gifts that every girl dreams of. The paying for my own birthday present from him. The hidden groping as I was talking to friends standing outside of a food truck on a busy street. The "I'm screwed up" approach to getting out of an argument.

No, he did not technically hit me. But he did abuse me. He would throw things all over the apartment. He would take pictures of me when I was sleeping. He would save articles of my clothing and display them on his walls. He would invade my space daily.

The final straw was the emergency room visit where the doctor told me that the "illness" that he had been trying to tell me that he got all of a sudden, was an alcohol addiction that he had been denying for the months that we lived together.

This is not to say that addiction is desired. I do not believe that he woke up one day wanting to put everyone around him in danger. I do not think he looked in the mirror one day and decided to throw away all his life into a bottle. His dreams were big. His goals were attainable. But he threw away his shot in a shot glass, all of it stripped away.

What I will say is that I felt like the biggest idiot. *He could have died.* I paid for some of his hospital bills and medication. I stayed the night in a cot next to him thinking that an enlarged liver was such a strange thing for a seemingly healthy man in his twenties to have. I prayed that he would not die.

But it was like everyone around me saw what I did not see. I did not see that the water bottle he was drinking from was full of vodka when we sat in church. I did not believe that his profuse sweating was caused by anything other than the pressure to impress my family.

I had no idea that the man in the hospital bed in front of me had a 0.34 BAC. I did not know. And, how could

I have? Why would I expect that? After all, the doctor two weeks before said that a glass of wine would likely kill him with his condition. The doctor that I had to chase as they wheeled him down the hall of the emergency room in a hospital bed, calling every nurse on staff since he appeared to be dying.

Why would he drink?

And better yet how was I to know? Was he drinking when he drove me places? Was he drinking when he kept dropping my dog? Was it because he was drunk that he would often stumble into his bed to tell me that he was sick?

It was after I told him "to find another ride home" from the hospital that things got worse. I immediately changed my relationship status on social media and went to get my belongings from his apartment.

For months after, he would call me. Sometimes 10 times a day he would call. He would send texts saying that he could not help it. That our relationship was actually the reason he drank. That he wanted to tell me what was going on, but that it never came up organically.

He would tell me to go on dates with him. And honestly, I felt obligated to go. After all, he did not choose his addiction.

He did not ask to be an addict.

Every morning, I would check the paper for his obituary.
What really needed a eulogy was my heart. In an instant,
my feelings ceased to exist. My empathy died.

I was jaded. Dead inside. Blocked off people, sharp as a tack
to burst any positive bubble in my life.

Today, I still pay the consequences. No interaction with
him for nearly 10 years, and I still seek negative attention.
I confuse a lack of physical intrusion for a lack of attraction.
The acts of respect seem like the intentions of indifference.

One person. One relationship. The world spun on its head as
my life fell to the floor. All I wanted was to be wanted. And at
the end, I didn't even know who I had become. This person
who craved attention no matter the cost. This girl who once
squeezed the potential out of every day suddenly could not
get out of bed in the morning.

And now, I have the most amazing boyfriend. Someone who
loves me so unconditionally. Someone who shattered all
expectations. Someone I did not believe existed.

No, I did not need someone to pick up my pieces. But he helps a lot.

If you can relate, you deserve more than the person who invisibly steals your dreams. You are worthy of someone who wipes your tears away and tells you how strong you are. Someone who loves you. And I mean, *truly* loves you.

And that person you need is you.

vines

Love is patient,
Love is kind,
How lucky I am,
That love is mine.

Love is tough,
Love is not easy,
Why do people,
Assume it would be.

Love is hugs,
Love is kisses,
We are individuals,
I am more than just his "Mrs."

Love is real,
Love is true,
My identity is not based,
On the moment I said, "I do."

Love is great,
Love is never-ending,
The expectations began,
The day of our wedding.

"Where is your husband?"
"Why are you keeping your last name?"
"When are you having kids?"
"Be sure to stay as thin as your wedding frame!"

Love is great,
Marriage is heavy.
Contrary to your beliefs,
Your opinions don't help me.

Lily

I stand with you,
I hear your truth.
I fight for you,
I will be your Ruth.

My story is not of bruises,
Of screaming or fighting or injustice.
My story is subtle,
But it is mine nevertheless.

Telling my story feels a bit strange.

A lot of women have amazing testimonies. The ones that overcame and tell of the times that they crawled out of abusive situations with the skinned knees and the bruises to prove it. Others have been kept from positions of power because of their gender identity, or not taken seriously because they are a woman. Like their sex somehow makes them weak, vulnerable, a target, or even stupid.

I listen to their stories. I live to stand in solidarity with these heroines—to hold their hand and pat their back and shout from the rooftops that women deserve all the rights of men, and that our voices should be heard.

And yet, when I sit and think about how my life has been affected by inequality, I cannot think of anything specific.

Sure, I have been catcalled. I have sat in a crowded subway and quickly thought of escape routes in the case that I was in danger. I follow the unwritten code of conduct for women: I have walked through a dark parking lot at night, fumbling for my keys to put one between my knuckles if I was attacked. I pretend to be on the phone when a stranger walks near me. I received pepper spray as a gift from my father when I started college on a large campus, and I reached for it just to have in my hand as I quickly made my way back to my dorm after my evening classes. All seemingly normal occurrences in the daily life of a woman.

Professionally, I work in a creative field. I am not in a male dominated field, but people do assume that my work is "fun" just because of its nature. Maybe it is easier to look in my eye and tell me to redo something. Maybe you can change your mind a million times and expect me to be patient with you because I am a woman. While I might be more patient and soft spoken, it is not right to assume that because of my gender.

As for my relationship, I have my person. But so often, people ask "where is your better half?" if he and I are not together at an event.

Which let me mention, I *hate* that phrase. He and I are complete people. We have individual gifts. We have skills that are unique from one another. We are people. People are not puzzle pieces that mosey throughout this world playing a never-ending and impossible game of hide-and-seek with their counterpart. I like to think of us as salt and pepper or peanut butter and jelly. We stand on our own but are better together.

We dated all through high school. He was two years older than me, so he went to college at the beginning of my Junior year. Suddenly, all the boys in my class saw me as a challenge. They made advances at me because he was not at school with me. They acted like, because they were in front of me, they were a better option. Some would say "he doesn't have to know; he isn't here."

Truthfully, none of those guys ever paid attention to me until I was not in the dating pool. Like they were waiting for the credibility of another man to say, "yeah, she's suitable" in a sort of Yelp-style review.

And yet, I worried that my boyfriend was dealing with the same thing. Would he resent me by staying with me? Am I enough for this college guy?

For whatever reason, the question of being enough is ever present in my life.

Is my work good enough? Do I need to look more like that model? Should I have accomplished more than I already have at my age? Do I need to go to more rallies and protests?

And yet the question that I keep getting asked is "when are you going to have kids?"

Are my goals and dreams even important if I have not met the expected goal of having kids? Am I considered complete without my husband?

Maybe I do belong here in this crowd of women begging for change. I do not have the cuts and bruises, but I do have a few suggestions.

So, men, get a pen and notebook and be ready to hear what I have to say. It's your turn to take notes.

epilogue

This book has been an ever-changing labor of love for nearly three years. As time has continued to pass, more and more stories have unfolded, and the buds bloomed.

When I first decided to write this book, I was in an incredibly confusing and bitter place. I had accepted a job working for a company where I realized that sexism was alive and well. The kind of sexism that I was warned about but believed existed as much as I believe in the Tooth Fairy or Santa Claus.

While I had assumed that sexism came from a place of not letting women vote or read, it stretches beyond policies and rules and into the words and assumptions of those around us.

Not asking the only woman in the room to take notes cannot be changed into a law.

Not assuming that your female coworker is menstruating cannot be fit into company policy.

Excluding women in your office from company golf outings or happy hour is not explicitly mentioned anywhere in the employee handbook.

And so, I began writing. I recollected any encounter that I had with sexism in the workplace. I created stories about women in relationships. I read between the lines of office gossip that I would hear outside the ladies' restroom. I listened to the stories of friends who struggled to find their place in this modern suffrage movement. I thought about what might have occurred if I stayed in a certain toxic relationship, or what could have happened if I never stood up for myself or if I had never listened to the people in my life who told me that I deserved better.

I sat on these diary-esque entries for about a year. I did not know when I would make these stories into a book. I think a lot of it had to do with what I thought of my own perception of feminism.

Growing up, I hated that word. It was simply another f-word.

Feminism jostled visions of men-hating women who demanded rights that they legally already had.

They wanted their voices heard, but I didn't understand why.

If you could legally do everything that a man can, why are you still fighting for rights? What injustices are you even talking about?

I did not know anything about the subtly loud injustices occurring. Like the price of women's razors over men's. The tabloid headlines that judged female politicians for what they wore instead of what they had accomplished. The constant lack of representation of women in rooms where women's rights are at risk.

But the first day that sexism struck me at work, hindsight suddenly became an eagle eye.

Your boss was not hitting on you; that was harassment.

Your ex-boyfriend did not really like you; he was using you.

Those guys on Facebook were not just joking; they did not respect your opinion because you are a woman.

You did not get hired because of your merit; you were hired because they needed more women.

While all of these stories are textbook scenarios of bias and sexism, I did not find my life relatable.

Unfortunately, it was very relatable.

In fact, I wish that everything that you had just read was not something that you could relate to—that each of these stories was some sort of twisted tale of what life would be if women were not taken seriously in the workplace. Like I just had a vividly wild imagination and that none of this was possible.

Not only is it possible; it is common.

There are three people in my life that had read this book in its purest form. And not even one of them ever tried to tell me that my stories were far-fetched. My story is not extraordinary or unique. It is not wildly uncommon or rare. It is the story of womankind. These flowers in *The Garden* are our mothers, sisters, aunts, cousins, mentors, and teachers. My garden is not a subsect of people from a small town, but of an entire planet for generations. The flowers are not all the same, but of different colors, scents, and ages. No one is immune to the bugs and pollution that can affect this garden of life.

You see, I am not a magnet for the sexist pigs of the earth. I am not someone who seeks out those who think of women as a lesser species.

Unfortunately, these people live among us. Men and women alike. The men who look down, and the women who choose to stoop to a level below the ceiling that they fear breaking. The men who focus on the differences in "superiority" based on a "make me a sandwich" level of brain cells, and the women who label other ladies as sluts or bimbos based on the style of their clothes or the pitch of their voice.

On a positive note, my experience is that those who do have these traits typically come from a place of ignorance and not of hate.

I do not fear ignorance. In fact, I often look for it. I love talking to people who were, like me, once incredibly uncomfortable with the word feminism. Those conversations can be a great opportunity to plant the seeds of knowledge in those that do not understand that it is truly a synonym for equality.

But it would be ignorant of me to ignore and not acknowledge the true and apparent bigotry and prejudice that rears its ugly head. It is real, and I will no longer deny its existence.

However, *The Garden* is not meant to create victims out of voiceless seeds, but to foster hope and solidarity for strong and firmly planted trailblazers.

I wanted to create something that provided a home. A garden is an incredibly beautiful but vulnerable place. People can look at the many different blooms and sprouts in awe. However, while some people look at flowers as delicate, there are constant threats to their ability to thrive. From wet weather to dry weather to novice green thumbs who pluck when they cannot tell the difference between a plant and a weed, flowers are resilient and can overcome many situations. Some bloom for the season and are replaced the next. Others bloom for one week and lie dormant until the following year. And others appear dead but are just waiting for the right gardener to come by to help it grow. No matter where you fit in, a garden has a spot for you to bloom.

I hope that this book encourages you. I hope that it finds you not only now as you read, but that it continues to bring you comfort. That you can pick it up next week or next year and find new meaning to each story. I pray that you find peace in its words, and that you can pass the stories along to others in your life who need it the most. That each flower meets you where you are, wherever you may be. That no matter how you bloom, *The Garden* is here to provide you a place to be watered, grow, and stand tall.

Reach for the Sun. Grow each time you are stomped. Stretch far and wide until you no longer can. And know that you are never alone.

thank you

I have many people to thank. From the women in my life to those who unintentionally inspired this book, none of this would be possible without you.

First, to the last three Taylor Swift albums for being my playlist as I write this book. From "If a man talks shit, then I owe him nothing" to "wondering if I'd get there quicker if I was a man", you truly are my muse. Here is to realizing that women's rights are worth more than our symbolic dollar bills. They are ownership of our bodies and our work.

Next, to my mom. Thank you for listening to me cry on numerous occasions and teaching me that women are capable of anything. You gave me my voice, and you empower me when I am sure it feels dangerous. You stand so close to my fire and proceed to pour gasoline on it, and I cannot thank you enough. You are the best and the first woman I met, and if I can be even half as strong as you, I will be happy.

Next, to my friend, Brittany. I have called you "Mom" for years, and yet life has made you more of my older sister. Thank you for our many conversations, late night texts, and for reading this book with a red pen in hand. Your knowledge of both grammar and life will always be appreciated.

Next, to my boyfriend, Ryan. When I stayed up into the wee hours of the night writing and we were on opposite schedules, you continued to encourage me. You taught me that it is as important to be respected as it is to be loved. Thank you for not being a chapter of this book.

Next, to my friend, Ashley. The only thing more beautiful than your illustrations for this book is our friendship. You served as a frequent bringer of homemade brownies and wine during some of these chapters and have been my heartbreak buddy for over ten years. Thank you for agreeing to be a part of this project and thank you for being a part of my life. My garden grows more beautiful with you in it.

And to my friend, Tess. Thank you for blindly agreeing to write for me. While states might keep us miles apart, your steadfast encouragement and well-crafted compliments made me want to finish this book faster so that more people could read it. From "good luck and keep strong" to "the fragrance of a flower in the unpolluted air", your presence in my life has been nothing short of a gift. Your foreword made me want to read my book, and I hope that it encouraged you to see the artist in yourself. I am thankful that no matter the miles we will continue to grow towards the same sun. Also, you are hardly a dandelion.

Thank you to each person reading this book. Whether you purchased your own copy, borrowed it from a friend, or stumbled upon it by accident, your support of my debut work will never go unnoticed or unappreciated.

Thank you.

about the author

Photo by Anna Powell Denton

Mackenzie Lynn was born and raised in a small town in southern Indiana. When she isn't writing or playing volleyball, Mackenzie is traveling or spending time with her friends, family, and her cat, Manning. *The Garden* is Mackenzie's debut book.

Mackenzie is available for panel discussions, keynote presentations, and workshops regarding women in the workplace. Visit mackenzielynnfreelance.com for inquiries and to subscribe to her newsletter.

@authormackenzielynn   @thinkdreamwrite